0500000641630 4

GLOUCESTER

Copyright © 2013 by Emily Arnold McCully
All Rights Reserved
HOLIDAY HOUSE is registered in the U.S. Patent and Trademark Office.
Printed and Bound in December 2013 at Tien Wah Press, Johor Bahru, Johor, Malaysia.
The artwork was created with pen and ink and watercolors.
www.holidayhouse.com
3 5 7 9 10 8 6 4 2

Library of Congress Cataloging-in-Publication Data
McCully, Emily Arnold.
Pete won't eat / by Emily Arnold McCully. — 1st ed.
p. cm. — (I like to read)
Summary: Pete the pig does not want to eat his slop, but cannot go
out to play with his brother and sisters until he does.
ISBN 978-0-8234-2853-3 (hardcover)
[1. Food habits—Fiction. 2. Pigs—Fiction.] I. Title. II. Title: Pete will not eat.
PZ7.M478415Pet 2013
[E]—dc23
2012039209

ISBN 978-0-8234-3183-0 (paperback)

Pete Won't Eat

by
Emily
Arnold
McCully

I Like to Read®

Holiday House / New York

"I made a treat,"
says Mom.

"Here it is—green slop."

Dot loves the slop.

Rose slurps the slop.

Gus has all of it.

But Pete won't eat.

"Slop is good," says Mom.
"No," says Pete.

"Try one bite,"
says Mom.
"No," says Pete.

"Eat your slop," say Dot, Rose, and Gus. "We want to go out and play."
"I won't!" says Pete.

"Dot, Rose, and Gus
may go," says Mom.
"I hate green,"
says Pete.

"Bye," says Dot.
"We will be in the yard,"
says Rose.

"You will stay until you eat," says Mom.

"I hope he tries it,"
says Mom.

"Yuck," says Pete.

"I want
to go out,"
says Pete.
"I want
to play."

"It's getting late,"
says Mom.

The kids call. "Come out and play."

"Please eat your slop, Pete," says Mom.

"I hate green slop,"
says Pete. "Poor me."

Mom cries.
"I am a mean mom!"

"I will make something Pete likes."

"I will make you a sandwich," says Mom.

Pete looks at the slop.
"How **does** it taste?"
says Pete.

"It's not bad."

"It's good!"
says Pete.

Mom sees Pete eat.
"No need for this,"
she says.

Now Pete can go out.
"Here I am!" says Pete.
"Let's play!"

The next day,
Pete and Mom
make more slop.

I Like to Read® Books
You will like all of them!

Visit holidayhouse.com to read more
about I Like to Read® Books.

I Like to Read® Books in Paperback
You will like all of them!

Boy, Bird, and Dog by David McPhail

Car Goes Far by Michael Garland

Come Back, Ben by Ann Hassett and John Hassett

Dinosaurs Don't, Dinosaurs Do by Steve Björkman

Fireman Fred by Lynn Rowe Reed

Fish Had a Wish by Michael Garland

The Fly Flew In by David Catrow

Happy Cat by Steve Henry

I Have a Garden by Bob Barner

I Will Try by Marilyn Janovitz

Late Nate in a Race by Emily Arnold McCully

The Lion and the Mice
    by Rebecca Emberley and Ed Emberley

Look! by Ted Lewin

Me Too! by Valeri Gorbachev

Mice on Ice
    by Rebecca Emberley and Ed Emberley

Pete Won't Eat by Emily Arnold McCully

Pig Has a Plan by Ethan Long

Sam and the Big Kids by Emily Arnold McCully

See Me Dig by Paul Meisel

See Me Run by Paul Meisel
    A THEODOR SEUSS GEISEL AWARD HONOR BOOK

Sick Day by David McPhail

What Am I? Where Am I? by Ted Lewin

You Can Do It! by Betsy Lewin

Visit http://www.holidayhouse.com/I-Like-to-Read/ for
more about I Like to Read® books, including flash cards,
reproducibles, and the complete list of titles.